LETTS

The Sea-Breeze Hotel

The Sea-Breeze Hotel

Marcia Vaughan & Patricia Mullins

HarperCollins*Publishers*Ltd

High on a cliff overlooking Blow-Me-Down Bay stood the Sea-Breeze Hotel. Mrs. Pearson ran the old hotel, with the help of Henry the handyman, Hilda the housekeeper, and Henry's grandson Sam.

The Sea-Breeze Hotel should have been bustling with happy holidaymakers. But no one wanted to stay there. It wasn't because of Mrs. Pearson, or Henry, or Hilda, or Sam. It was the fault of the wind.

From out of the south blew a boisterous, blustery breeze that blasted and buffeted the hotel for eleven months of the year.

"It's too windy to fish and swim," moaned the children.

"It's far too breezy for beachcombing," the parents complained.

"It's even too blustery to sit on the balcony," the grandparents grumbled.

And they all packed their bags and went away.

"What are we going to do?" sighed Mrs. Pearson, looking at the empty guest book. "Unless the wind stops blowing, we'll have to close."

It was seeing Mrs. Pearson looking so sad that gave Sam an idea.

Down in the cellar he found just what he needed—
a broken fishing rod, fishing line, and scraps of cloth
left over from the kitchen curtains.

Then he started to work.

He cut the cloth into the right shape, stitched the seams,
painted a big, bright face, and attached two feather
boas very securely to the trunk.

When his surprise was ready, he gave it to Mrs. Pearson, who was sitting on the balcony all bundled up in her winter woollies.

"A kite! For me?" she gasped. "I haven't flown a kite in fifty-two years. I don't think I even remember how. . . ."

Just then a gust of wind snatched the kite out of her hands
and hurried it up and up into the sky.

Dipping and whirling, spinning and swirling, that kite danced above their heads.

"Whee!" shouted Mrs. Pearson. "This is the most fun I've had in years."

"If we're not going to have any guests," Henry said, watching Mrs. Pearson's kite play tag with the sea gulls, "we might as well all make kites and have some fun."

So Hilda made a butterfly kite.

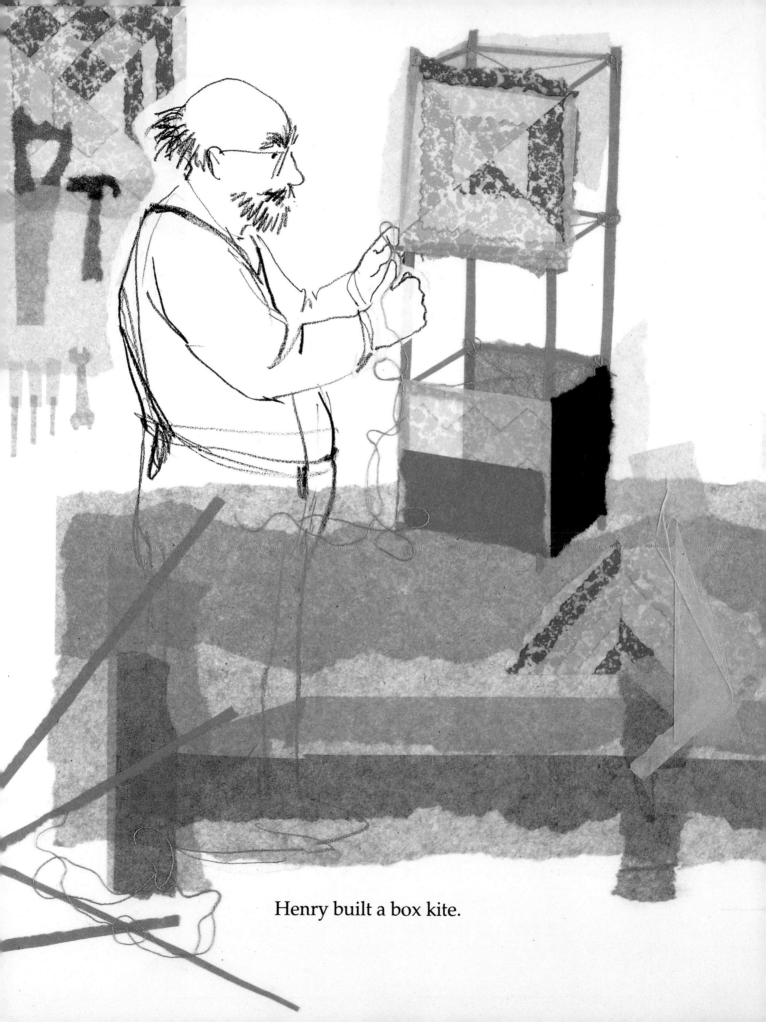

Henry built a box kite.

Sam designed a dragon kite with a long green tail.

Together they flew their kites until their arms were almost
too tired to hold on.

People began to notice the four kites circling and soaring in the sky above the Sea-Breeze Hotel.

Girls and boys and mothers and fathers and aunts and uncles and grandmas and grandpas all came hurrying up the hill to join in the fun.

"Is there any of that fishing line left," Mrs. Pearson
asked, "and wood and scraps of cloth?"

"Lots," said Sam.

"Then let's get busy. We've got kites to make, and
plenty of them," she declared.

And make kites they did. Blue ones, red ones,
green ones, and gold ones. Round kites, square kites,
big kites, and kid kites. Kites with stripes and stars
and dots. They made lots and lots and *lots* of kites.

When people heard about the kite-flying hotel
they came from near and far.

Children ran up the beach pulling their kites.

Parents stood on the cliff.

Aunts and uncles and grandmas and grandpas leaned
way out over the railing.

The sky all around the Sea-Breeze Hotel was alive with
kites.

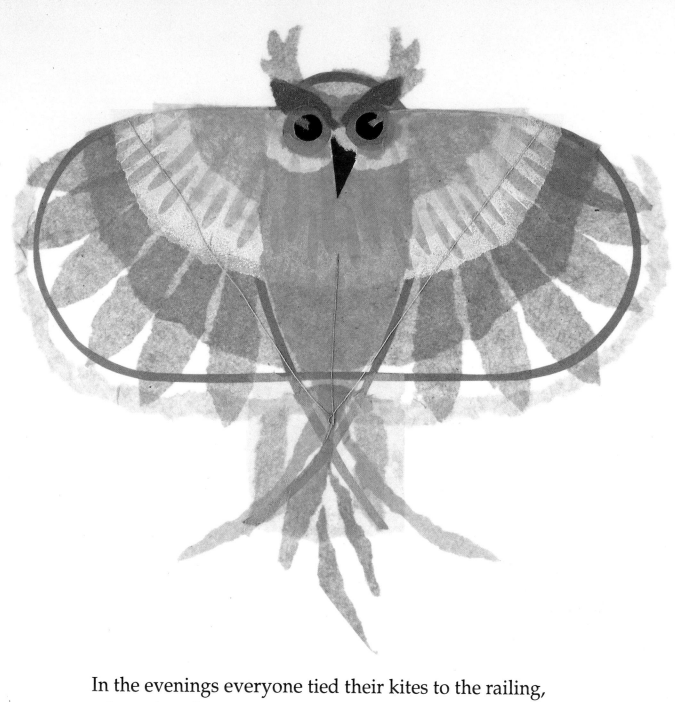

In the evenings everyone tied their kites to the railing,
where they flew all night in the moonlight.

Not one person complained about the wind. Best of all,
the Sea-Breeze Hotel was full all the time.

Except in April, when the sea breeze hushed to a whisper, and the hotel stood empty.

It was then that Henry and Hilda and Mrs. Pearson and Sam were busy swimming and fishing and combing the beach for seashells.

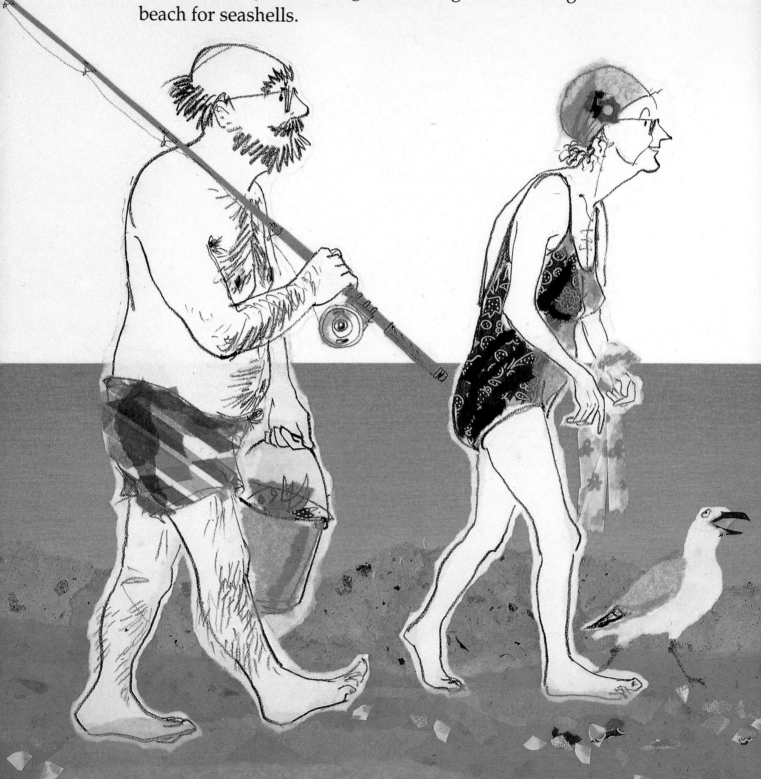

And making plenty of new kites for the busy year ahead!

Canadian Cataloguing in Publication Data

Vaughan, Marcia K.
    The Sea-Breeze Hotel

1st Canadian ed.
ISBN 0-00-223888-8

I. Mullins, Patricia, 1952-   . II. Title.

PZ7.V38Se   1992   j823   C91-095642-1

The Sea-Breeze Hotel
Copyright © 1992 by Marcia Vaughan and Patricia Mullins
First published in 1991 by Margaret Hamilton Books Pty Ltd, Australia
HarperCollins*Publishers*Ltd. Toronto. All rights reserved.
1 2 3 4 5 6 7 8 9 10
First Canadian Edition, 1992

The illustrations were created as torn-tissue collage and reproduced
from photographs by Bob Peters, Sydney. The text was set in 15/20
Palatino by Silver Hammer Graphics. The book was printed and
bound in Hong Kong.